THE Berenstain BEAR SCOUTS

Save That
Backscratcher

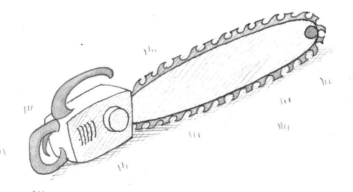

THE Berenstain BEAR SCOUTS

Save That
Backscratcher

by Stan & Jan Berenstain
Illustrated by Michael Berenstain

A
LITTLE APPLE
PAPERBACK

SCHOLASTIC INC.
New York   Toronto   London   Auckland   Sydney

No part of this publication may be reproduced in whole or in part, or stored in a retrieval system, or transmitted in any form or by any means, electronic, mechanical, photocopying, recording, or otherwise, without written permission of the publisher. For information regarding permission, write to Scholastic Inc., 555 Broadway, New York, NY 10012.

ISBN 0-590-60382-5

12 11 10 9 8 7 6 5 4 3 2 1   6 7 8 9/9 0 1/0

Printed in the U.S.A.   40

First Scholastic printing, February 1996

• Table of Contents •

THE Berenstain BEAR SCOUTS

Save That
Backscratcher

• Chapter 1 •

A Good Scratch

The Bear Scouts were in high spirits as they tooled along on their way to Scout Leader Jane's. Brother was roaring along on his skateboard. Sister was on her bike. Fred and Lizzy were rollerblading. They had some great ideas for their next merit badge. In fact, they had too many. They'd been arguing about whether to go for the Whitewater Rafting Badge, the Wilderness Camping Badge, or the Scuba Diving Badge. But Scout Leader Jane would help them decide.

"Hey!" called Scout Brother as they

sped along. "We've got plenty of time. Let's stop off at the town square and touch base with Gramps."

The funny thing was that the town "square" was a circle — a traffic circle around a small park. It was a pleasant place where folks liked to pass the time of day. There were benches, some statues, and a great tree that had been there as long as anyone could remember.

GENERAL GRIZZWELL

The park was set among Beartown's most important buildings: the town hall (the mayor's office was on the second floor), the town library, and the police station and lockup.

But, say, who's that going into the mayor's special entrance? Why, it's none other than Ralph Ripoff, Beartown's leading crook and swindler. Some folks, including Gramps, think that Ralph should be in the lockup instead of making regular visits to see the mayor.

But, be that as it may, it was Gramps's habit to visit the little park at the same time every day. There he would sit on his favorite bench in the shade of the great tree and read the afternoon paper. The tree, a shagbark hickory, was the oldest tree in Bear Country. It was a famous landmark, though nobody thought much about it anymore — except oldsters like Gramps. A brass plate in the ground told the story of "Old Shag." But it was over-grown with weeds.

Gramps truly enjoyed his daily visits to the little park. There wasn't much traffic, and what there was was kind of lazy. The heavy traffic used the main highway and took the bypass around Beartown. Though Gramps was enjoying the quiet and the shade of the great tree, he wasn't enjoying his afternoon paper very much. He was, in fact, finding it quite irritating. Especially the front-page headline, which said, "Mayor Honeypot to Run Unopposed Once Again."

"Humph," grumped Gramps. "High-and-mighty Honeypot! Somebody *should* run against him. Maybe that'd get him down off his high horse."

Gramps went on to read the story that went with the headline. But he was inter-rupted by a loud noise. The noise was a cross between a roar and a rumble, and it

was peppered with bicycle-horn honks and shouts of "Gramps! Gramps! Watch this!" It was the skateboarding, bicycling, rollerblading Bear Scouts. They were bearing down on Old Shag. Gramps picked up his feet as they roared past.

They put on quite a show. They did wheelies and twirlies and jumps and bumps as they circled the huge tree. They nicked its roots in a couple of places and knocked off a piece of its shaggy bark.

Gramps was furious. He leaped up, shouting, "Stop it! Stop it! That's Old Shag you're dealing with! Try to show a little respect!"

The scouts stopped in their tracks. They were puzzled and confused. "Old Shag?" said Sister.

"That's right," said Gramps. "Old Shag's just about the most important tree in Bear Country. It goes back hundreds of years. Old Shag stands for something."

"Gee, we're sorry," said Brother.

"We didn't mean any harm," said Sister.

"I guess not," said Gramps, calming down a bit.

"We were on our way to Scout Leader Jane's. We just thought we'd stop by and say hello," said Fred.

"And show you some of the stunts we can do," said Lizzy.

Gramps picked up the piece of bark and pressed it back into place. "There," he said. "Almost as good as new. Well, it was right thoughtful of you to stop by. I appreciate it. Going to Scout Leader Jane's, you say? Well, be off with you. Give her my regards."

"Will do," said Brother. "Let's go, troop."

As the scouts sped off, Gramps turned

to the tree and said, "They're good cubs, old friend. But you just can't expect cubs to understand some things." Then he leaned his back into the tree and gave himself a good scratch.

• Chapter 2 •

Shocking News

The Bear Scouts were still bubbling with high spirits and excitement when they arrived at Scout Leader Jane's. But they wouldn't be for long.

It seemed dark in the house after the bright sunlight. So the scouts couldn't see that Jane wasn't her usual smiling self. The scouts were chattering about Bear Scout plans and projects as usual. But Jane stopped them. Their eyes had gotten used to the dark, so they could see that Jane was serious. But they couldn't in a million years have guessed what she was about to say.

"Scouts," she said. "I have an important announcement to make. I have resigned from my Bear Scout duties. I am no longer your scout leader."

The scouts couldn't have been more surprised if Scout Leader Jane had told them she was running for mayor. That was the next thing she told them.

"The reason I am resigning is that I'm running for mayor." With that, she picked up a big roll of paper with a rubber band around it. She removed the rubber band and let it unroll. It was an election poster. It said, "Jane for Mayor."

The scouts understood Jane's words

well enough. But that was all they understood. The idea that Jane would no longer be their leader was shocking and upsetting. It was like having the rug pulled out from under you, like slipping on an icy spot that didn't look icy, like reaching for a step that wasn't there.

It was no wonder the scouts were upset. Jane had been their leader from the beginning. The scouts liked her. They liked her a lot. What they liked most about her was that she didn't fuss at them about every little thing. She trusted them. She let them choose their own merit badges, do their own good deeds. She didn't even seem to mind that they kept their clubhouse a secret.

Jane could read the shock and disappointment in their faces — and the questions. "Of course, you're wondering who your next scout leader will be," she said.

"Well, I'm very glad to tell you that my good friend and fellow teacher, Miss Stickler, has agreed to be your new scout leader."

Jane went on to say a lot more. She said that it had been great being their leader, that she was sure they would do well under their new leader, and that she would miss them. But the Bear Scouts hardly heard her. As it happened, the scouts knew Miss Stickler, though only by reputation. And that reputation was, to put it mildly, a little scary. She taught at the middle school. The rumors about her were that she was . . . well, a stickler: a stickler on grammar, on spelling, on punctuation, on just about everything a teacher can be a stickler about.

The scouts were still lost in thought when they heard Jane say, "Well, are there any questions?" The scouts may have had some, but word had gotten around and the phone started ringing. Jane was kept busy answering it. "Jane for Mayor headquarters, Jane speaking," she said. "I couldn't agree with you more. Our present mayor has been in office much too long . . . I agree about that, too. His relationship with Ralph Ripoff is something we all should be worried about . . . er, would you excuse me for just a moment?" Jane turned to the scouts. "You can let yourselves out, scouts. You're to be at Miss Stickler's tomorrow at three o'clock sharp. Be on time. She's a stickler on punctuality. That's her address on my notepad — and good luck!"

Jane was still on the phone as the scouts let themselves out. Brother was staring at Miss Stickler's address. "Well," he said, "maybe this Miss Stickler won't be as bad as we expect."

Scout Brother was right. Miss Stickler wasn't as bad as they expected. She was much worse.

• Chapter 3 •

Stickler, the Stickler

"That's just gossip and rumor," said Brother.

The Bear Scouts were hurrying to their first meeting with their new scout leader.

"It's not gossip and rumor," said Lizzy. "My cousin Jill goes to middle school, and she says Miss Stickler is the toughest teacher in the whole school. She's a stickler on everything: grammar, spelling, punctuation, manners, posture — *everything!*"

"I heard she gave a cub fifty pages of extra homework for saying 'who' when he should have said 'whom,'" said Fred.

"I heard she kept a cub after school for dotting her *i*'s with little circles," said Sister.

"I heard she made a cub stand in the corner for *slouching*," said Lizzy.

The scouts had reached Miss Stickler's house. "All right! That's enough!" said Brother. "She's going to be our scout leader, and there's nothing we can do about it. So let's try to keep an open mind." He reached up and pressed the doorbell.

"Is that anything like a hole in the head?" said Sister.

The scouts didn't have to wait long. The door popped open before the *ding-dong* inside faded away. And there stood Miss Stickler, the scouts' new leader. She wore harlequin glasses, bangle bracelets, dangle earrings, and a big wide smile with lots of teeth. She didn't look much like a witch, and her house certainly wasn't a candy cottage. But as she stood beaming down at them as if they were chocolate cupcakes with jimmies, they began to feel like Hansel and Gretel.

After giving her watch a quick look, she said, "Names, please!" Then, as the scouts sounded off, she said, "This way, troop!" and led the Bear Scouts into her den.

"Stickler's the name," she said, facing the scouts, "and dealing with cubs is my game. I don't know what you've heard about me. But whatever it is, it's all true. I've got eyes in the back of my head. I can hear the grass grow, and I've got more rules than a dog has fleas. As you may have heard, I'm a stickler about certain things. I'm a stickler about being punctual, for example. You were thirty seconds late. Don't let it happen again. I'm a stickler about posture. You with the glasses. You're slouching," she said, pointing at Fred. He straightened up so hard, his hat fell off.

"I am also, it happens, a stickler about uniforms. So when you put your hat back on, do it properly."

"Properly?" said Fred, picking up his hat.

"And that goes for the rest of you, too!" said Miss Stickler. "Your hats are at more angles than a bunch of Frisbees in the wind." She opened the *Official Bear Scout Handbook.* "'The Bear Scout hat,'" she read, "'shall be worn with the brim straight across and positioned exactly the width of two fingers above the eyebrows.'"

The scouts busied themselves fixing their hats. Especially Scout Lizzy, who was in the habit of wearing hers hanging off the back of her head by the chin strap.

"And while we're on the subject of uniforms," Miss Stickler continued, "your neckerchiefs look like refugees from a rag bin."

The scouts got busy straightening their neckerchiefs.

"And why in the world," said Miss Stickler, pointing at Lizzy, "are your pant legs rolled up?"

"Well," said Lizzy, "we were down by the river because we're planning on going for the Whitewater Rafting Badge. I was wading. So I rolled up my pant legs."

"You can forget about rafting, Lizzy," said Sister, "because Fred and I voted for wilderness camping."

"Forget about wilderness camping," said Brother. "It's the Scuba Diving Badge we're going for."

"Forget all three," said Miss Stickler. "I'm the only one around here whose vote counts, and I vote for the History Merit Badge."

The History Merit Badge? The scouts had never even heard of the History Merit Badge!

• Chapter 4 •

From Bad to Worse

The scouts opened their mouths to protest. But no sound came. It wouldn't have mattered if it had. Because there was no stopping Miss Stickler.

"I happen to be a stickler on history," she said, reopening the *Official Bear Scout Handbook*. "So I was delighted to find this in the appendix. Fred, I understand you read the dictionary just for fun. Define *appendix*."

"*A-p-pendix*," said Fred, a little shaken up. "Pronounced a-PEN-dix: *a short tube in the lower right-hand side of the abdomen*. Its purpose . . ."

A-p-pendix...

"Not *that* appendix," said Miss Stickler.

"Huh? Oh," said Fred. "*Appendix: extra material at the end of a book.*"

"Here in the appendix of the *Official Bear*

Scout Handbook — a short tube indeed! — under 'Advanced Merit Badges,'" said Miss Stickler, "are some *wonderful* merit badges. Why, here's the English Usage Merit Badge and the Poetry Merit Badge. And, best of all, the History Merit Badge! It's a wonder to me that you haven't gone for these before instead of all that nonsense about whitewater rafting and the like."

The scouts were becoming more and more discouraged. What did English, poetry, and history have to do with scouting?

Miss Stickler went on for quite a while. "Well," she said finally. "Is all that understood? You will submit your ideas on the History Merit Badge as soon as possible. And, oh yes — I'm starting a demerit program. It will work as follows. Crooked hat, one demerit; sloppy neckerchief, one demerit; pant legs rolled up, two demerits."

There was no question about it. Things were going from bad to worse.

"The meeting is adjourned," said Miss Stickler. "Come! My car's just outside."

The scouts were surprised. "Gee, thanks," said Brother. "But you don't have to drive us home."

"Drive you home?" said Miss Stickler. "Don't be ridiculous. I understand you have a clubhouse. I shall have to inspect it, of course."

"But our clubhouse is a secret!" protested Brother.

"That's right!" said Sister.

"Nobody knows where it is!" said Fred.

"Not even Scout Leader Jane!" said Lizzy.

"*You* know where it is," said Miss Stickler. "Into the car, please."

• Chapter 5 •

Miss Stickler's Way
or the Highway

There was no arguing with Miss Stickler. It was her way or the highway. In this case it was the highway that led past the Bear Scouts' secret chicken coop clubhouse at the far edge of Farmer Ben's farm.

"There it is," said Brother.

It was Miss Stickler's turn to be shocked. "You mean that awful-looking, falling-down mess is your clubhouse?"

Miss Stickler didn't like the Bear Scouts' chicken coop clubhouse one bit. She didn't like the way it looked. She didn't like the way it smelled. (The scouts tried to explain that it had smelled a lot worse before they cleaned it up.) She didn't like it being a secret. She didn't like anything about it. It wasn't long before they were in the car heading back to Miss Stickler's.

"We certainly are going to have to do something about that clubhouse," said Miss Stickler as they drove along. "But don't worry. It's amazing what you can do

with a little paint, some curtains, and a few geraniums. Inside, an air freshener wouldn't hurt at all," she added, wrinkling her nose.

"All right," said Miss Stickler when they got back to her house. "Remember to get back to me with your History Merit Badge ideas as soon as possible."

The scouts headed home in silence.

Sister was the first to speak. "Remember," she said, "when you said Miss Stickler was going to be our scout leader and there was nothing we could do about it? Well, you were wrong. There *is* something we can do about it. We can quit."

Quit. The very word was shocking. It hung in the air as they walked along in silence. It followed them home.

• Chapter 6 •

A Big Decision

"Quit the scouts?" said Gramps. "You can't be the same scouts that came roaring through here full of beans and ready to lick the world the other day."

It was the day after the first meeting with Miss Stickler. The Bear Scouts were sitting with Gramps on his favorite bench in the shade of the most important tree in Bear Country.

The Bear Scouts sighed.

"We're the same scouts, Gramps," said Brother.

The troop had decided to sleep on the

idea of quitting. Now they were doing
what they often did when they faced a big
decision. They were touching base with
Gramps.

"*Those* scouts," said Gramps, "had spirit
and grit. Those scouts wouldn't even *think*
of quitting just because they got a new
scout leader."

Just then a pickup truck stopped at the
edge of the park. The driver got out and

walked over to the big tree. He leaned his back into it and gave himself a good scratch. "Phew!" he said. "I really needed that." Then he got back into his truck and drove away.

"Gee, Gramps," said Brother. "What would *you* do if someone took over your secret clubhouse, told you how to wear your hat, and made you go for the History Merit Badge?"

"I'll tell you what I *wouldn't* do," said Gramps. "I wouldn't quit."

"But, Gramps," said Sister. "Scouting isn't about history. It's about whitewater rafting, wilderness camping, and scuba diving. Everybody knows that history is just a lot of boring dates and hard-to-remember names."

"It's funny that you should say that sitting here in this little park in the shade of Old Shag."

"What's the park and some old tree

have to do with it?" said Brother.

"This park," said Gramps, "and that 'old tree,' as you call it, are history. History isn't just a bunch of names and dates. History is *what happened!* It's everything that took place to make us what we are today."

That's when Farmer Ben pulled up in his hay wagon. As he climbed down from the wagon, he saw Gramps and the scouts.

"Hi, scouts," he said. "Who was that lady I saw you with at your clubhouse yesterday?"

"That was no lady," said Brother. "That was our new scout leader."

Farmer Ben leaned his back into Old Shag and scratched hard.

"You know, it's kinda funny," he said, as he climbed back onto his wagon. "My back doesn't usually itch that much. But when I see Old Shag, it itches like crazy. Well, see you!" said Ben as he drove away.

"Farmer Ben comes by here fairly often," said Gramps, "sometimes with Mrs. Ben. Yessir, Old Shag means a lot to Bear Country folk. Come with me." Gramps got up from the bench and took Scouts Sister and Lizzy by the hand. Brother and Fred followed along. "You see that statue over there?"

It was a statue of a soldier on a horse. Of course the scouts saw it. They'd seen it many times before. But they had never thought much about it.

"That's General Stonewall Grizzwell," said Gramps. "And that other one is General Ulysses S. Bruin. They were the opposing generals in the Great Bear War."

"Yes," said Fred, who read the encyclopedia, as well as the dictionary, just for fun. "I think I've read about them in the encyclopedia."

"I don't doubt it," said Gramps. "Now, come over here." He led them back to Old Shag. He leaned down and brushed the weeds away from the brass plate at the foot of the tree. "All right," ordered Gramps. "One of you read that out loud. And *then* tell me that history's just a bunch of boring names and dates."

"'Old Shag,'" said Brother, reading aloud. "'Generals Grizzwell and Bruin brought the Great Bear War to an end by signing the peace treaty under this great tree.'

"Wow!" said Brother.

"Gee!" said Sister.

"Very impressive," said Fred.

"Totally awesome," said Lizzy.

"And then," said Gramps, "they sealed the bargain by scratching their backs on the rough bark of this great shagbark hickory. As did all the members of their parties: colonels, majors, captains, right down to second lieutenants."

"It must have been quite a scene," said Brother.

"It must have been," said Gramps. "And since then," he continued, "just about every important bear in the history of Bear Country has come here and scratched on Old Shag. Because when you scratch your back on Old Shag, you're scratching it on history."

The scouts could almost see the great historic scene in their mind's eye.

"Scouts," said Gramps. "Aren't your backs beginning to itch just a little?"

"Yes!" said the scouts, almost as one. "They're beginning to itch a lot!"

"Then what are we waiting for?" cried Gramps. "Let's tune in to history! Let's scratch!"

"Ooh! Ah! Oh!" cried the scouts as they scratched and scratched and scratched.

"I wonder," said Scout Brother, when they'd finished scratching, "whether Miss

Stickler would let us do our History Merit
Badge about Old Shag."

"Well," said Gramps, "it's certainly
something to think about."

• Chapter 7 •

Mr. Mayor, You're in Big Trouble

Perhaps Ralph Ripoff should have been in the town lockup for some of the tricks and swindles he had pulled on his fellow bears. But he wasn't. He was, in fact, in Mayor Honeypot's office, trying to convince him that he was in big trouble.

"There's no doubt about it, Mr. Mayor!" said Ralph. "You're in big trouble."

"Ralph, my fear dellow — er, dear fellow," said the mayor, who sometimes got the fronts and backs of his words mixed up. "I deg to biffer — er, beg to differ. I shall win this election. I shall win it woing

44

agay — er, going away! And the reason is that I am close to the people, the people hold me in great steam — er, great esteem."

"Mr. Mayor," said Ralph. "May I speak frankly?"

"My all beans — er, by all means," said the mayor.

"Mayor," said Ralph, "you haven't been close to the people since you got that mile-long purple limousine you and Mrs. Honeypot ride around in. You haven't been close to the people since Mrs. Honeypot started

MY ALL BEANS — ER, BY ALL MEANS.

carrying that pink parasol and wearing her glasses on a ribbon."

"Even if that were so," said the mayor, "I won't lose. I *can't* lose, *because nobody is running against me.*"

"But that is not so, Mr. Mayor," said Ralph. "I repeat: not, not, not so."

"*N-n-not so?*" said the mayor.

Ralph picked up a big roll of paper and let it unroll. It was a copy of Jane's election poster. The mayor, who had been standing behind his big, important-looking desk, fell back into his chair. "But . . . but . . . but," he sputtered.

"Jane says you have been in office too long," said Ralph.

"That durts me heeply — er, hurts me deeply," said the mayor.

"She says you have lost touch with the people," said Ralph.

"An arrow heep in my deart — er, deep in my heart!" cried the mayor.

"And that isn't the worst of it," said
Ralph. "She's going to start running TV
commercials tomorrow. Here's one I got
through my spies — er, friends — at the
TV station."

Ralph popped a cassette into the
mayor's VCR. He pushed the power but-
ton. Some words came up on the screen.
They said, "Break up the Gang of Two!"

"Tang of Goo — er, Gang of Two," said
the mayor. "Who are they?"

As if in answer, the faces of none other
than the mayor and Ralph Ripoff came up
on the screen. "We give you Honeypot and
Ripoff, the Gang of Two," said the voice on
the TV. It then went on to tell about some
of the crooked schemes Ralph and the

mayor had almost gotten away with.

"But those were *your* ideas, Ralph!" protested the mayor.

"Which I freely admit," said Ralph. "That is why I will bend every effort, go the last mile, to get you reelected. My card, sir."

Mayor Honeypot took the card. It said, "Ralph Ripoff, Election Advisor."

"A little company I have formed," said Ralph.

"What do you advise, Ralph?" said the mayor. "What can I do to get back close to the people?"

"It's too late for that, Mr. Mayor," said Ralph. "You could junk the limo and take away Mrs. Honeypot's parasol. But it wouldn't do any good. No, you've got to do something big, something grand, something that will blow Jane out of the water!"

"What do you suggest?" said the mayor.

Quick as a flash, Ralph reached into an oversized briefcase and took out a folded easel and a flip chart. Then, quicker than a flash, he set up the easel and flip chart. "What I suggest is the Horace J. Honeypot Super-Duper Six-Lane Highway."

That's what it said in big bold letters on the cover of the flip chart.

"Mell me tore — er, tell me more," said the mayor.

• Chapter 8 •

Slogan Time

Meanwhile, down in the park, Gramps and the Bear Scouts were sitting in the shade of Old Shag, eating ice-cream-on-a-stick. Gramps had bought ice cream from the Good Humor Bear. It was to celebrate the troop's decision not to quit scouting. There was no way Miss Stickler or anyone else could drive them out of scouting. Not if they stuck together.

"Save your sticks," said Brother.

"I didn't know you collected ice-cream sticks," said Fred.

"I don't," said Brother, holding out his stick.

The rest of the troop got the message. It was slogan time. Gramps looked on with pride as the scouts crossed sticks and shouted, "One for all, and all for one!"

But the scouts were still worried about Miss Stickler.

"Gramps," said Brother, "I'm not sure Miss Stickler will like the idea of a history project about a . . . well, about a back-scratcher."

"I don't see why not," said Gramps. "Everybody likes a good scratch now and then."

"I don't know about that," said Fred. "I don't think Miss Stickler is the sort of bear who itches."

Just then a van drove up and some election workers got out. They were carrying folding tables and some papers. On the side of the truck it said, "Jane for Mayor!"

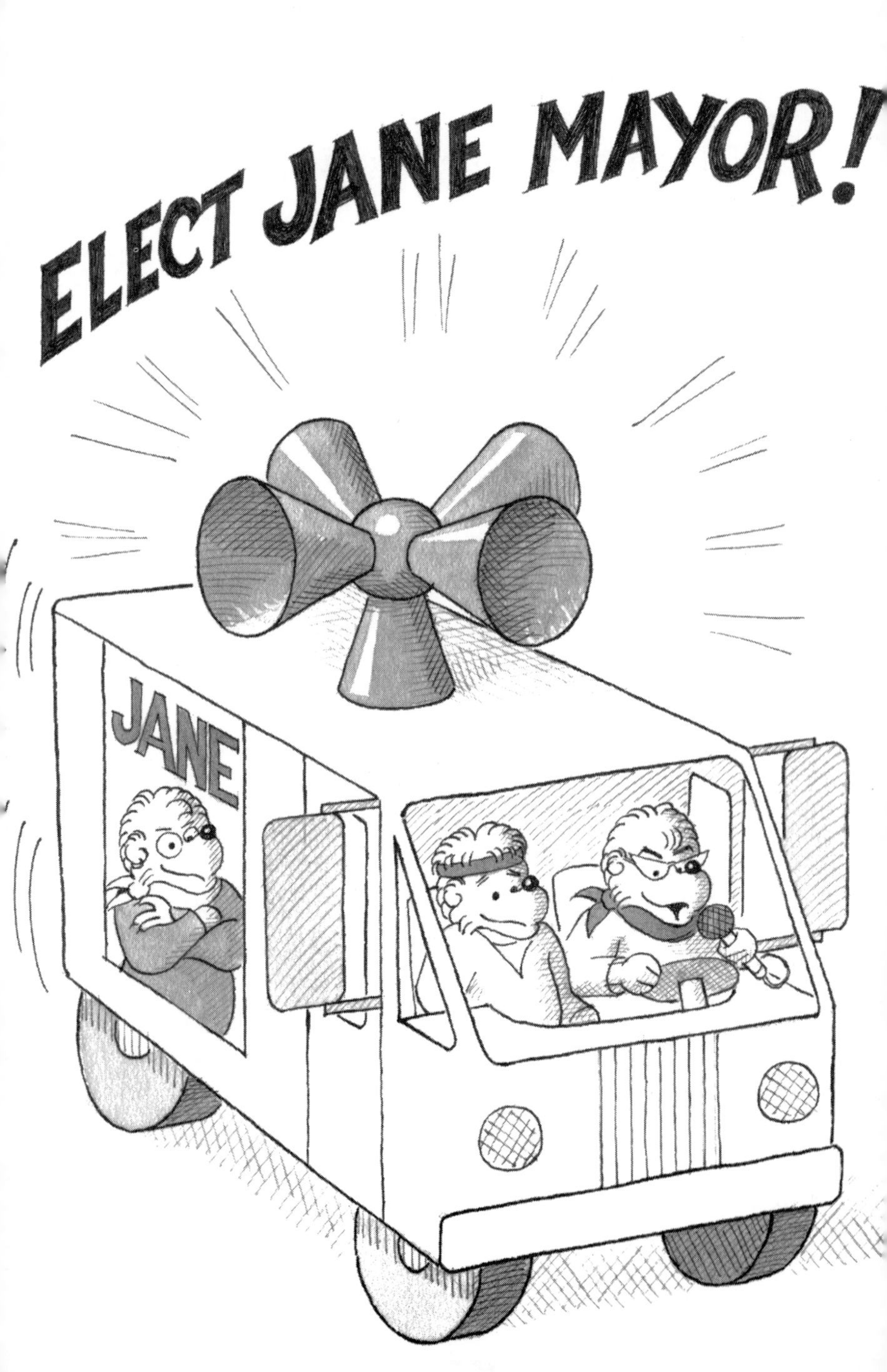
ELECT JANE MAYOR!
JANE

The van had a loudspeaker. *"Elect Jane mayor!"* it blared. *"Break up the Gang of Two! Sign our petitions!"*

"I'd know that voice anywhere," said Brother. "It's Miss Stickler!"

Sure enough it was.

"I'd like to meet her," said Gramps. "And now's your chance to talk her into the Old Shag Merit Badge."

"Good idea!" said Brother. "Let's go, scouts."

"Hold it," said Fred. "Don't you think we ought to get our uniform act together first? You know — hats, neckerchiefs."

The scouts fixed themselves up a bit. Then they headed for the van.

"Why, it's my scout troop!" said Miss Stickler. "What are you doing here?"

"Gramps would like to meet you," said Brother.

"And," said Sister, "we'd like to tell you about our History Merit Badge idea."

"Fine with me," said Miss Stickler. She had another worker take over the loud-speaker and went with the scouts.

"Miss Stickler," said Brother, "we'd like you to meet Gramps."

"Delighted, sir," said Miss Stickler.

"And I," said Gramps, "would like you to meet Old Shag."

Miss Stickler was confused. "Old Shag?" she said.

"Yes," said Gramps. "Old Shag is this great tree."

"That's right," said Brother. "We want to do our History Merit Badge about Old Shag."

"Well, it certainly is a handsome tree," said Miss Stickler. "But I am at a loss as to what it has to do with history."

"Why, Old Shag *is* history!" said Gramps. "Here, have a look at this!" He pointed at the brass plate in the ground. Miss Stickler read it.

"Hmm," she said. "I do remember something about this tree. An important treaty was signed under it."

"That's right, ma'am. General Stonewall Grizzwell and Ulysses S. Bruin — those are their statues right over there — signed the treaty ending the Great Bear War under this tree."

The scouts could tell Miss Stickler was impressed.

"And then," continued Gramps, "after they signed the treaty, they sealed the bargain with a good scratch."

"Scratch?" said Miss Stickler.

"That's right," said Gramps. "Because Old Shag is not just a great historic tree. It's a great backscratcher."

"I don't quite understand," said Miss Stickler.

At that moment a big, burly truck driver, who had just parked his six-wheeler, came over.

"'Scuse me, folks," he said. "But I've been on the road for hours and I itch real bad!" Then he leaned his back into Old Shag and scratched like crazy. "Ooh! Ah! Oh! Ooh!" he shouted as he scratched.

"Oh, dear!" said Miss Stickler.

The big truck driver finally stopped. "Terrific scratch," he said. "You ought to try it, lady."

"I, sir," said Miss Stickler, "do not itch."

"It's your funeral," said the truck driver as he left.

"Well!" said Miss Stickler, a little shaken. "I suppose it's all right for you to do your History Merit Badge on this backscra — er, this great historic tree. Now, if you'll excuse me, I must get back to my election duties."

"See, I told you she didn't itch," said Fred.

• Chapter 9 •

Highway Robbery

"It moggles the bind — er, boggles the mind," said Mayor Honeypot.

Ralph's plan was boldness itself. It was to replace the traffic circle and the little park with the Horace J. Honeypot Super-Duper Six-Lane Highway.

"Mr. Mayor," said Ralph. "I am proud to say that this will be the biggest ripoff — er, project — of my career. It will mean jobs, excitement. It will be big news all over Bear Country."

"I can see the upside: jobs, excitement, big news," said the mayor. "But what's the downside?"

"The downside is that if you don't do this," said Ralph, "Jane is going to beat you like a drum."

"I like your idea, Ralph," said the mayor. "I like it a lot. It's a real dumhinger — er, humdinger! But tell me. Who's going to build this ripoff — er, highway?"

Ralph whipped out another card. This one said, "Ralph Ripoff, Road Builder."

"Gee, Ralph," said the mayor. "I didn't know you knew anything about building roads."

"Roads are in my blood, Mr. Mayor," said Ralph. "I come from a long line of road builders. My great-uncle, Asphalt Ripoff, built roads all over the world. And his great-uncle, Pothole Ripoff, invented the detour!"

"Won't a six-lane highway through the center of town create a nottlebeck — er, bottleneck?"

RALPH RIPOFF,
TRAFFIC JAMS
ON DEMAND.

"No, sir!" said Ralph. "It's our old-fashioned traffic circle that causes traffic jams."

"Jaffic trams — er, traffic jams," said the mayor. "I've never seen any traffic jams."

"You will, Mr. Mayor. You will." Ralph leaned in close. "My card," he said.

This one said, "Ralph Ripoff, Traffic Jams on Demand."

"Have a look at this." Ralph handed Honeypot a flier. "Hundreds of these will be spread around town."

The flier said, "Present this at the traffic circle and get a free gift."

"What will they get?" said the mayor.

"One of these." Ralph took a balloon out of his pocket and blew it up. It said, "Honk for Honeypot."

"It will be the biggest, noisiest traffic jam Beartown has ever seen," said Ralph.

"I've got to hand it to you," said the mayor. "It looks like you've left no turn unstoned — er, no stone unturned. But tell me. Won't this all cost a lot of money?"

"A *whole* lot of money," said Ralph, leaning in even closer. "My card." This one said, "Ralph Ripoff, Highway Robbery." "That's the beauty part. Please let me explain."

The mayor kept a big jar of coins on his desk. Ralph seized the jar and dumped it right in the middle of the desk. Then he plunged his hand into the pile of coins. As he lifted it out, he let the coins fall back into the pile — *except for the ones that were stuck between his fingers!*

"Do you really think we can get away with — er, convince the voters that the Horace J. Honeypot superhighway is a good thing?"

"We'd better," said Ralph. "Come over here and look out the window, Mr. Mayor."

What the mayor saw made him swallow hard. The little park below was a beehive of "Elect Jane" activity. The Jane for Mayor loudspeaker was going full blast. Folks were lined up around the corner to sign Jane for Mayor petitions.

The mayor sighed. "What will happen to that old tree?" he said.

"Old Shag? It will have to be destroyed, of course," said Ralph. "Well, Mr. Mayor. Is it a 'go'?"

The mayor sighed again. "It's a go," he said.

• Chapter 10 •

This Tree Is Condemned

"Hey! What are you scouts doing down there?"

The scouts looked up to see Officer Marguerite frowning down at them.

"Well?" she said. "I'm waiting for an answer." She was carrying something under her arm.

"We're making a rubbing of this brass plate at the foot of Old Shag," said Brother. He held up the rubbing. It was only half finished.

"Rubbing? Old Shag?" Officer Marguerite leaned forward. "Many's the time

I've scratched my back on this old tree. I didn't even know it had a name. Never noticed this brass plate before, either."

"How about that!" she said, after she read it. "Tell me about this rubbing."

"Well," said Sister, putting the half-finished rubbing back on the plate. "You place the paper so. Then you hold the pencil sort of sideways and rub gently — it has to be gently so you won't break the pencil point or tear the paper."

"You could use a crayon," said Fred. "Or an art pencil with big thick lead. It tells how to do it in the *Official Bear Scout Handbook*."

Sister was still at work.

"This rubbing," said Officer Marguerite. "What's it for?"

"It's for a Bear Scout merit badge — a *History* Merit Badge," said Fred. "You see, we have this new scout leader, Miss Stickler, and . . ."

"Miss Stickler?" said Marguerite. "I had her in middle school. Talk about tough. She caught me chewing gum once. Made me chew that same piece of gum for a week. My jaws are *still* tired. History, you say. What are you going to do with the rubbing?"

"Our History Merit Badge project is going to be a big album," said Fred. "It's going to have all kinds of history stuff in it: this rubbing, photographs, maps, old letters, whatever."

"There's plenty of history around here," said Marguerite. "There's no doubt about that. See that statue over there? That's General Stonewall Grizzwell. He was my great-grandfather on my mother's side. My mother's a Grizzwell. His name's right there in the old Grizzwell family Bible."

"Do you think maybe we could make a copy of the page with his name?"

"Don't see why not," said Marguerite.

"I'm a Bruin," said Lizzy. "My dad says that other general, Ulysses S. Bruin, was my great-great-grandfather."

"How about that," said Officer Marguerite, looking at the little park with all its history. "Just think. Your great-great and my great signed a big peace treaty under this big old tree."

"And then they scratched their backs on it to seal the bargain," said Fred.

"So they say. So they say," said Marguerite. She looked around the little park again. "You know something?" she said. "I'm glad you're doing this. That album will be a good thing to have when this old tree is gone. What did you say its name was?"

"Old Shag," said Brother. "What do you mean, 'gone'?"

"Just what I said," said Marguerite. "This tree is condemned." With that, she hung the sign she'd been carrying on Old Shag. The sign said, "This tree is con-

71

demned — by order of Horace J. Honeypot, Mayor."

"Condemned?" said Sister. "What's that mean?"

"It means they're going to take it down and grind it up into sawdust."

"What?" cried the scouts.

"Yep. Tomorrow afternoon at exactly two o'clock," said Marguerite. "The mayor's going to be here, Mrs. Honeypot, TV cameras, the works. Going to be a big deal. Mayor's going to cut a ribbon for the new highway. Well, see ya."

The Bear Scouts were stunned. They could almost hear the growl of the chainsaw as it cut down Old Shag and the awful roar of the chipping machine as it ground Old Shag into sawdust.

• Chapter 11 •

Emergency Meeting

"This emergency meeting of the Bear Scout troop will come to order," said Miss Stickler. "Be it noted that Gramps, a friend of scouting, is also . . ."

"Never mind all that," said Gramps, breaking in. "Let's get down to business! They're gonna murder Old Shag, and we gotta stop 'em!"

"Calm down, Gramps," said Brother. "Miss Stickler is on *our* side."

"Thank you, Brother," said Miss Stickler. "Gramps, I am a stickler for rules. I insist that this meeting be run by the

rules in the *Official Bear Scout Handbook.*
The floor is now open for suggestions as to
how to save Old Shag."

Brother raised his hand.

"Brother has the floor," said Miss Stickler. But Gramps broke in again.

"Never mind all this fancy-pants floor
nonsense," said Gramps. "You want a suggestion? I'll give you a suggestion! I suggest that the first thing we gotta do is run
that no-account crook, Ralph Ripoff, out of
town! He's the one at the bottom of all this
superhighway nonsense! Horace Honeypot
hasn't got the *brains* to . . ."

"GRAMPS, IF YOU PLEASE!" said
Miss Stickler.

"Please calm down, Gramps," said Sister. "We know you're upset. But shouting
at Miss Stickler isn't going to help Old
Shag."

"Thank you, Sister," said Miss Stickler.
"As I was saying, Brother has the floor."

"Here's what I was thinking," said Brother. "Aren't there laws protecting things that are part of history? Maybe there's some law that'll protect Old Shag."

"It's a good thought," said Miss Stickler. "I checked and, yes, there is such a law. It's meant to protect buildings. As far as I could find out, it does not protect trees. Not even a tree as important as Old Shag." Lizzy raised her hand. "Yes, Lizzy. You have the floor."

"What about all the animals who live in Old Shag?" said Lizzy. "There must be hundreds of squirrels, birds, and insects who live in Old Shag. They'll all be homeless if . . ."

"I don't believe this!" cried Gramps. "They're gonna grind Old Shag into sawdust and we're still sittin' here talkin' about squirrels and birds and bugs. Well, count me out! I'm leavin'! I know Horace Honeypot! Before he got so high-and-

mighty, we used to be friends. Me and
Gran and him and Hannah used to double-
date. We used to go fishing together. We
used to scratch our backs together. You
can go on with your meeting. But I'm leav-
ing. I'm going out to his house and give

him a good talking-to. And if that doesn't work, I'm gonna give him a good shaking. And if that doesn't work, I'm gonna give him one of these!" Gramps held up a bony fist.

Gramps was almost out the door when Brother grabbed him. "Wait, Gramps," said Brother. "I may have an idea. You say you and the mayor were friends?"

"We were buddies," said Gramps.

"And you used to scratch your backs together on Old Shag?" said Brother.

"Sure. Where else?" said Gramps. "But that was a long time ago."

The scouts, Gramps, and Miss Stickler listened as Brother told them his idea.

"Hmm," said Gramps.

"Hmm," said Sister.

"Hmm," said Fred.

"Hmm," said Lizzy.

"You know something?" said Miss Stickler. "It just might work."

• Chapter 12 •

Ooh! Ah! Oh! Ah!

All was in readiness for the big ribbon-
cutting. Gramps, Miss Stickler, and the
Bear Scouts got to the traffic circle park
with time to spare. At first it looked as

though they might not get in. The park was roped off so that there was only one entrance. And you had to have tickets. That was something they hadn't counted on. If they didn't get in, they couldn't save Old Shag. They could see the chainsaw crew and the chipping machine at the edge of the park.

The scouts had seen chipping machines in action. Farmer Ben had one. He used it when he cleared scrub. It ate whole trees the way rats eat cheese.

Luckily, the Bear Scouts' friend Officer Marguerite was taking tickets. She let them in without any. She certainly had been right when she said this was going to be a big deal. A crowd was beginning to gather in the park. An even bigger crowd was gathering in the grandstands placed around the traffic circle. There were TV cameras all over the place. There was even a TV remote truck from Big Bear City.

There was a big yellow ribbon stretched across the park. This was where the highway was going to go. The mayor would cut the ribbon. Then the crowd would cheer for his reelection. At least, that was what was supposed to happen.

Gramps, Miss Stickler, and the scouts didn't stay together. As they moved among the crowd, they were careful to stay out of the way of Ralph Ripoff. Ralph was handing out Honeypot for Mayor signs. He didn't know Miss Stickler. But he knew Gramps and the cubs all too well.

They couldn't be sure their plan would work. But to carry it out, they would have to be close to Old Shag when the mayor made his speech and cut the ribbon. They worked their way closer and closer. The "condemned" sign was still hanging on the grand old tree. They could hear the sound of the chainsaws being tested. They could see the big orange chipper waiting for its dinner.

The crowd stirred. The mayor and Mrs. Honeypot were arriving in the purple limousine. The TV cameras turned toward them. Ralph held up a big applause sign. There was some applause. Mrs. Honeypot was carrying a pink parasol and wearing her glasses on a ribbon. There was a

SAVE OLD SHAG! SAVE OLD SHAG! SAVE OLD SHAG!
THIS TREE IS CONDEMNED by order of Horace J. Honeypot, Mayor.

speaker's platform with a microphone. The Honeypots mounted the platform. The mayor came to the microphone. He raised his arms to the crowd. There was a little more applause.

The chainsaws were at the ready. The mayor was about to speak, but before he could start, six members of the crowd sprang into action. They were Gramps, Miss Stickler, and the scouts, of course. Before anyone could stop them, they had thrown their backs against Old Shag. With arms linked, they made a chain around the great tree and began to chant, "Save Old Shag! Save Old Shag! Save Old Shag!"

All the TV cameras turned toward them.

"What in the world do you think you're doing?" shouted the mayor.

"We're calling you home, Horace!" cried Gramps. "We're calling you back to yourself, old friend!"

The mayor recognized Gramps. "Look, Hannah," said the mayor. "It's our old friend Ernest!"

By this time the crowd had taken up the cry. "Save Old Shag! Save Old Shag!"

"I didn't know your name was Ernest," said Brother.

"Have them arrested!" said Mrs. Honeypot.

"Doesn't your back itch just a little?" called Gramps, as he scratched his back on Old Shag. "Oh, that feels good!" cried Gramps. "Doesn't it itch *just a little*, Horace?"

"Why, yes." The mayor reached over his shoulder to scratch. "Why, yes, it does. Just a little."

"Then, come on down!" cried Gramps.

The mayor leaped down from the platform and threw his back against Old Shag. "Yes! Yes!" he cried. "It itches a lot! Yes! Yes! Ooh! Ah! Yiii! Oh! Ah! Ooh!"

The crowd stopped chanting and began to cheer the mayor. This time, for real.

"Come, Hannah. There's nothing like it! Ooh! Ah!" cried the mayor.

Mrs. Honeypot hesitated for a moment. But then she threw away her parasol, leaped from the platform, and put *her* back into it. "Mmm! Ah! Oh! Oh!"

The cameras rolled. The crowd roared. A good scratch was had by all. Even Miss Stickler sneaked a bit of a scratch when she thought no one was looking.

Finally, the mayor stopped scratching.

He mounted the platform, raised his arms for quiet, and said, "The Horace J. Honeypot Super-Duper Six-Lane Highway is hereby cancelled!"

The roar of the crowd was tremendous.

They had done it. Their plan had worked. Old Shag was saved.

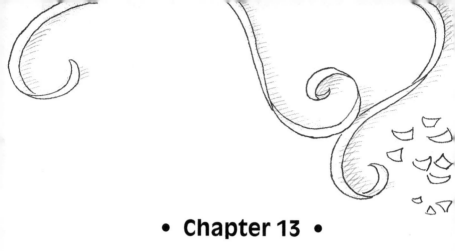

• Chapter 13 •

Jane's Return

As it turned out, Mayor Honeypot won the election. It was close. But Honeypot won. Some said he won because he had so many relatives and some of them may have voted twice. But Gramps didn't agree with that. Gramps thought it was because the mayor had gotten back to his roots,

because he'd gotten down off his high horse and scratched his back. "Folks identify with that," said Gramps. "Everybody needs a good scratch now and then. Even folks who 'don't itch,'" he added with a wink.

It wasn't easy for Jane, of course. Nobody likes to lose. But she was glad she had run. At least she had broken up the Gang of Two. It was reported that when last seen, Ralph Ripoff was out on the main highway selling balloons.

Candidate Jane was also very glad to get back to being Scout Leader Jane. The Bear Scouts were *very* glad to have her back. Not that they didn't appreciate Miss Stickler. She was tough. But they had learned a lot from her — especially about history. They were proud to have earned the History Merit Badge. They were very proud that the album they had made — it was called "Old Shag: A History" — had

been put in the Beartown Library for all
to see.

The Bear Scouts were at their first
meeting since Scout Leader Jane's return.

"Jane," said Brother, "we've been having
an argument about which merit badge to
go for next: the Whitewater Badge, the

Wilderness Badge, or the Scuba Diving Badge."

"I'm not in favor of any of those," said Jane. "The badge I want to go for is the 'Just Relax and Have Fun Badge'!"

"But there is no such badge," said Sister.

"There is now," said Jane with a grin.

So that's what the scouts did. They just relaxed and had fun for a while. They skateboarded. They bicycled. They rollerbladed. And every so often, they stopped for a good scratch.

• About the Authors •

Stan and Jan Berenstain have been writing and illustrating books about bears for more than thirty years. Their very first book about the Bear Scout characters was published in 1967. Through the years the Bear Scouts have done their best to defend the weak, catch the crooked, joust against the unjust, and rally against rottenness of all kinds. In fact, the scouts have done such a great job of living up to the Bear Scout Oath, the authors say, that "they deserve a series of their own."

Stan and Jan Berenstain live in Bucks County, Pennsylvania. They have two sons, Michael and Leo, and four grandchildren. Michael is an artist, and Leo is a writer. Michael did the pictures in this book.

Don't miss

THE Berenstain BEAR SCOUTS

and the
TERRIBLE TALKING TERMITE

"I'm down here!" said the voice. Ralph looked down. What he saw was so weird and frightening that he would have jumped into his own arms if he'd known how.

There, standing on a rock at the base of the post that held up the mailbox, was an enormous bug! Ralph tried to speak. But he'd lost his voice. When he found it, all he could do was stutter, "Wh-wh-what in the S-S-Sam Hill are you?"

"Sam Hill has nothing to do with it. But

it's a reasonable question. And since I *am* a bit hungry, I'll show you." With that, the giant bug scurried over to a log and ate it. There was a noise like a buzz saw, and before you could say Terrible Talking Termite, the log had turned into a pile of sawdust.

"Y-y-you're a termite," said Ralph.

"I am indeed," said the creature. "Woody's my name, and mine is a strange and sad story. Would you like to hear it?"

"I'm all ears," said Ralph. He was not only all ears, he was atwitter with excitement as well. He was putting together that phone call about insurance with this amazing buzz saw of a giant termite. A combination of the two might be just what he was looking for: a really big con.

THE Berenstain BEAR® SCOUTS
by Stan & Jan Berenstain

Join Scouts Brother, Sister, Fred, and Lizzy as they defend the weak, catch the crooked, joust against the unjust, and rally against rottenness of all kinds!

Collect all the books in this great new series!

Don't miss the Berenstain Bear Scouts' other exciting adventures!